Glenwood Springs Branch Library
413 9th Street
Glenwood Springs, CO 81601
(970) 945-5958 Fax (970) 945-7723
www.garfieldlibraries.org

Sarah Wilson

Big Day on the River

illustrated by Randy Cecil

Henry Holt and Company • New York

Henry Holt and Company, LLC
Publishers since 1866
115 West 18th Street
New York, New York 10011
www.henryholt.com

Henry Holt is a registered trademark of Henry Holt and Company, LLC
Text copyright © 2003 by Sarah Wilson
Illustrations copyright © 2003 by Randy Cecil
All rights reserved.
Distributed in Canada by H. B. Fenn and Company Ltd.

Library of Congress Cataloging-in-Publication Data
Wilson, Sarah.
Big day on the river / Sarah Wilson; illustrated by Randy Cecil.
Summary: Willie's relatives bring her so many provisions for her
rafting trip that she almost does not get to go.
[1. Rafting (Sports)—Fiction. 2. Family life—Fiction.] I. Cecil, Randy, ill. II. Title.
PZ7.W6986 Bi 2003   [E]—dc21   2002004358

ISBN 0-8050-6787-6 / First Edition—2003
The artist used acrylic gouache to create the illustrations for this book.
Printed in the United States of America on acid-free paper. ∞
1 3 5 7 9 10 8 6 4 2

For all of the Rochester Remingtons,
with love
—S. W.

For Pat Melton. Thank you.
—R. C.

At dawn, Willie danced her way to the river, joyful to be alone and grinning ear-to-ear.

"Yow-eee!" she shouted. "My first day out on the Wallawatchee, and nobody's here to tell me what to do or how to do it!"

Skinny-legs-tall, eyes sparkling, she ran down Uncle Buster's old dock and lowered herself to the little raft bobbing at the end. *Whump!*

"Off-we-go-dee-o," she sang.

The day was a dazzle. Bright sun, no wind, and the river like a sky mirror with hardly a ripple.

Suddenly she heard a loud shout.

"Hold up, Willie-Child," Gramma Clementia gasped as she hustled toward the raft. "It's a long-toed river out there. You'll be hungry as a hound by midmorning!"

Then she dropped a bumpy bag of apples at Willie's feet.

Willie gave her a big smile.

"Thank you, Gramma Clemmie," she said.

Gramma Emmaline huffed and puffed up the dock with a huge plump watermelon.

"In case you run out of apples, dear," she explained.

The watermelon was heavier than a full-grown raccoon in a washtub.

Still, Willie managed a smile.

"Thank you, Gramma Em," she said.

Grampa Jebediah brought Willie an umbrella as tall as a beanpole.

"You'll need this for a sun shade," he told her. "And, say, if a few old socks fall out when you open it, just stuff them in your backpack."

"Old socks?" Willie's nose twitched, but she nodded politely.

"Thank you, Grampa Jeb," she said.

Grampa Ezekiel stepped forward with a scratchy-looking blanket.

"Your arms'll get ice-bumps in the shade!" he said, throwing the blanket over Willie's shoulders. "Pay no mind to the horse hairs."

Willie gulped.

"Thank you, Grampa Zeke," she said.

Uncle Binderbus brought Willie her bicycle. "So you can wheel off to see the sights whenever you pull up to shore!" he exclaimed. It was no easy job to wrangle the bike onto the raft without falling—*splunk*—in the water.

But Willie held her tongue.

"Thank you, Uncle Buster," she said.

Wherever was she going to stand, much less sit?

Then Uncle Mumpford lowered
a heavy chair to the raft.

"Best cat-cuddling chair I ever
had," he told Willie, "but *you* need a
perch, Sugar Bean."

Willie looked at her raft and sighed.

"Thank you, Uncle Mumpfy," she said.

Aunt Josie-Beth and Aunt Katherine gave Willie a whopping big picnic basket and not one but two thermos bottles. "Lemonade for midday," they explained. "And hot chocolate in case you get caught under a cloud cover!"

Willie took a *very* deep breath.

"Thank you, Aunt Jay-B and Aunt Katie," she said.

Suddenly her feet started sloshing inside her boots.

Whompers!

Still, Cousin Luther plunked a camp stove down beside her.
And Cousin Clyde quickly topped it with a four-pound pot
of his mother's best baked beans.
"Now, *that's* what I call a well-stocked raft," he boomed.
"On your feet, Willie-Salt. Looks like you're going
to need help getting your gear under way!"
"No, WAIT!!!" Willie hollered, but he
was too far away to hear.

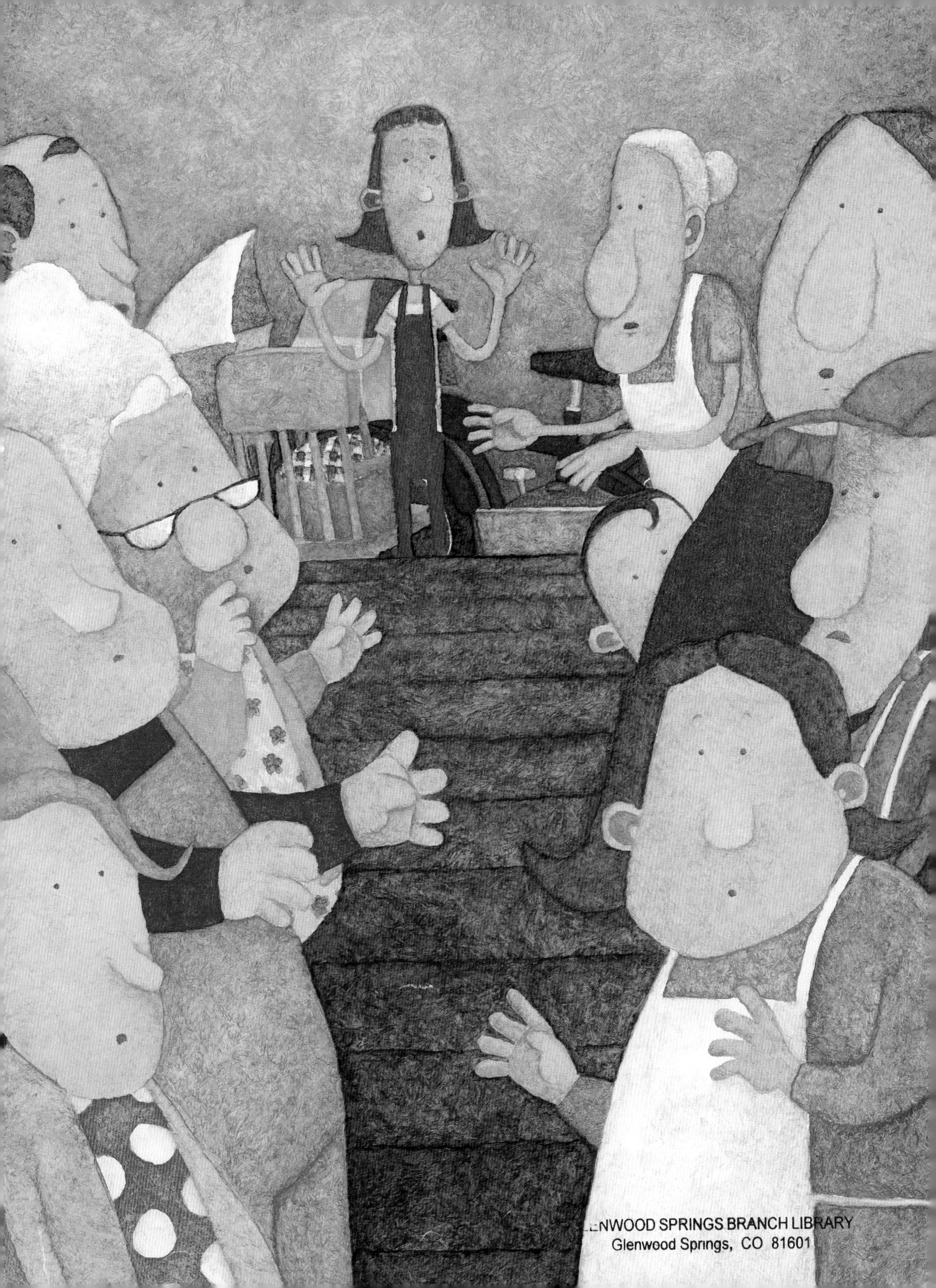

Cousin Clyde gave himself a running start, shot over the dock like a cow riding a cannonball, and landed,

THONK!

Willie's little raft promptly sank.

Suddenly, up bobbed the raft, swept clean as the day it was first lashed together.

Willie and Cousin Clyde popped up next in a wash of apples and beans. The two of them were laughing fit to burst.

The screeching stopped cold-crackers.

Then Gramma Em spotted her giant watermelon floating downriver. "I won *third prize* for that melon!" she shouted, yanking Uncle Mumpfy into the water.

Splossssh!

"I WANT MY SOCK UMBRELLA!" cried Grampa Jeb.
"Don't worry, Willie, *I'll* save your bike!" yelled Uncle Buster.
And in they all went, every last one of them, shouting and
splashing like happy otters. Fortunately, the water was
shoulder-high-shallow for a family of swimmers.

Everybody finally straggled back to shore with their rescued flotsam, drooping and dripping and looking sad-perplexed. All eyes turned to Willie.

"Your nice raft ride's slockered," wailed Gramma Em.

"No, no, no!" Willie said. "I love you all to popping, but *please* take back these wondrous things! All I *really* need . . .

. . . are your hugs, your kisses, and your *very* best wishes!" she told them.

"Those you have, Willie-Child," mumbled Gramma Clemmie, dabbing her eyes with Grampa Zeke's wet shirttail.

"ALWAYS!" shouted everybody else. There was a sunburst of smiles.

So, greatly hugged and lightly packed, Willie launched her raft out on the Wallawatchee.

At last.